MySELF Bookshelf

Nicknames

By Cecil Kim
Illustrated by SooJin Han
Language Arts Consultant: Joy Cowley

NORWOOD HOUSE PRESS

Chicago, Illinois

DEAR CAREGIVER   MySELF ▊▊▊ Bookshelf is a series of books that support children's social emotional learning. SEL has been proven to promote not only the development of self-awareness, responsibility, and positive relationships, but also academic achievement.

Current research reveals that the part of the brain that manages emotion is directly connected to the part of the brain that is used in cognitive tasks, such as: problem solving, logic, reasoning, and critical thinking—all of which are at the heart of learning.

SEL is also directly linked to what are referred to as 21st Century Skills: collaboration, communication, creativity, and critical thinking. MySELF Bookshelf offers an early start that will help children build the competencies for success in school and life.

In these delightful books, young children practice early reading skills while learning how to manage their own feelings and how to be considerate of other perspectives. Each book focuses on aspects of SEL that help children develop social competence that will benefit them in their relationships with others as well as in their school success. The charming characters in the stories model positive traits such as: responsibility, goal setting, determination, patience, and celebrating differences. At the end of each story, you will find a letter that highlights the positive traits and an activity or discussion to help your child apply SEL to his or her own life.

Above all, the most important part of the reading experience is to have fun and enjoy it!

Sincerely,

Shannon Cannon

Shannon Cannon, Ph.D.
Literacy and SEL Consultant

Norwood House Press • P.O. Box 316598 • Chicago, Illinois 60631
For more information about Norwood House Press please visit our website at www.norwoodhousepress.com or call 866-565-2900.

Shannon Cannon – Literacy and SEL Consultant
Joy Cowley – English Language Arts Consultant
Mary Lindeen – Consulting Editor

Library of Congress Cataloging-in-Publication Data
　Kim, Cecil.
　Nicknames / by Cecil Kim ; illustrated by SooJin Han.
　pages cm. -- (MySelf bookshelf)
　Summary: "Some nicknames can be mean and hurtful. When little Rabbit is called mean names, his feelings are hurt. Instead of using mean nicknames, he chooses to give his friends nice nicknames and in return the animals become nicer and more helpful"-- Provided by publisher.
　ISBN 978-1-59953-664-4 (library edition : alk. paper) -- ISBN 978-1-60357-724-3 (ebook)
　[1. Nicknames--Fiction. 2. Kindness--Fiction. 3. Rabbits--Fiction. 4. Animals--Fiction.] I. Han, SooJin (illustrator), illustrator. II. Title.
　PZ7.K55958Ni 2015
　[E]--dc23
　　　　　　　　　　　　　2014030341

Manufactured in the United States of America in Stevens Point, Wisconsin.
263N—122014

4

One sunny day,
a little rabbit hopped along,
feeling very happy.

But a fox and a racoon
made fun of him.
"Look at his big feet!
Hey, Big Foot!" they said.

When the little rabbit munched a carrot,
the fox and the raccoon appeared again.
"Look at how his teeth stick out!
Hey, Big Tooth!"

The little rabbit was angry.
His ears stood straight up.

"Ha ha!" cried the fox and raccoon.
"Look at his ears! Hey, Trumpet Ears!"

The little rabbit sat by the pond
and looked at his reflection.
"It is true. I have big feet,
big teeth and big ears."
He felt sad and started to cry.

9

Grandmother sat the little rabbit on her lap.

"Don't be sad," she told him.

"Your big feet and big ears

help you avoid danger.

Your big teeth help you

munch on crunchy foods.

These are things to be happy about."

The little rabbit smiled.

"Grandmother, you are right!"

A few days later, the little rabbit saw
the fox and the raccoon arguing.

The fox said to the raccoon,
"You are so ugly! Look at you!
You've got black glasses on your face."

That made the raccoon mad.
"How dare you call me ugly!
I'm not playing with you, Trickster!"

14

The little rabbit thought about this.
Bad names made friends feel bad.
Bad names made friends fight.
What they needed were good names.

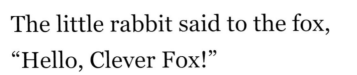

The little rabbit said to the fox,
"Hello, Clever Fox!"

16

To the raccoon, the little rabbit said,
"Hi, Handsome Raccoon."

The fox was surprised.
"Why do you call me Clever Fox?
My nickname is Trickster."

"You're smart," said the little rabbit.
"You have a lot of intelligence."

The raccoon was also surprised.
"Why am I Handsome Raccoon?
My nickname is Ugly One."

"You look as though you are wearing
cool black glasses and a stylish grey suit,"
said the little rabbit.

Then a strange thing happened.
The fox was no longer a trickster.
He became very clever.
The raccoon did not look ugly.
He acted like a handsome gentleman.
The fox, the raccoon and the little rabbit
became very good friends.

The clever fox had an idea.
"Why don't we give good nicknames
to our other friends in the forest?"

So the little rabbit, the raccoon
and the fox put their heads together.

"Squirrel works so hard.
He gathers food and saves it."

"Bear has such a good heart.
He never gets angry.
What are good nicknames for Squirrel and Bear?"

"Woodpecker knows everything that happens in the forest."

"Mole digs the best holes.
He has a good underground home."

"Warthog is very strong.
He can roll huge rocks."

"What are good nicknames for them?"

The little rabbit, fox and raccoon
thought of some good nicknames
for their friends.

"Angel Bear! You have a good heart."
"Busy Squirrel! You gather a lot of food."
"Wise Woodpecker! You know everyone in the forest."
"Builder Mole! You made another home today."
"Powerful Warthog! You are so strong and brave."

The next day,
the little rabbit was with his grandmother
when he heard someone call out to him.
"Noble Rabbit! Noble Rabbit!
Come and play with us!"

"What does *Noble Rabbit* mean?"
the little rabbit asked his friends.

"It means you are a kind rabbit
who is good to everyone," they said.

The little rabbit smiled.
He really, really liked his new noble nickname.

Dear Little Rabbit,

I was so pleased to hear all about the good nicknames you thought of for your friends. You and I have often talked about how words can be used to help others or hurt others, and now I know that you were really listening well with your big beautiful ears when we talked about that!

Every day we can choose how to use our words. We can choose to use them wisely or foolishly. You used your words very wisely when you found nicknames for your friends that named something good about each one. What a smart little rabbit you are!

Your friends also chose their words wisely when they nicknamed you Noble Rabbit. Your words and actions are careful, thoughtful, and fair. That is very noble thinking indeed.

With lots of love,
Grandmother Rabbit

SOCIAL AND EMOTIONAL LEARNING FOCUS

Kindness

Nicknames can be fun, but they can also be hurtful. Little Rabbit helped others by giving them positive nicknames. Sometimes grown-ups put their nicknames on the license plates of their cars.

You can design license plates for all of the members of your family—your friends too!

- Use a piece of 8 ½ x 11 inch paper and lay it out horizontally.

- Cut the corners to give them a rounded edge.

- Use a hole-punch to cut four holes (two at the top, two at the bottom).

- If you want it to be stronger, ask an adult to cut pieces of cardboard for you.

- Create a border around the paper.

- Write the positive nickname in big letters or numbers (real license plates usually only have up to 7 characters).

- Create a design for the license plate.

If you love to sing, yours might look something like this:

Reader's Theater

Reader's Theater is an interactive approach to reading that allows students to understand each story through dramatic interpretation. By involving students in reading, listening, and speaking activities, they provide an integrated approach for students to develop fluency and comprehension. A Reader's Theater edition of this book is available online. You can access the script by scanning the QR code to the right or visit our website at: http://www.norwoodhousepress.com/nicknames.aspx